"Failure is the mother of success."

- Chinese Proverb

Published by KTANG LIMITED.

First Printing

Garrett Bear

Learning From Failure

by K. Tang

Once upon a time, in Character Jungle, there lived a joyful bear named Garrett.

For the past couple months, he had just one **goal** – to become a **rock climbing champion**.

But he wasn't his joyful self today because he didn't win the rock climbing contest on Sports Day.

He did not reach his goal.

He dragged his feet back home and cried in Mama's Bear arms.

"Oh, I'm so sorry to hear that, baby." Mama said gently.

"Keep trying. I'm sure you'll do better next time." She encouraged Garrett.

"No Mama, I don't want to rock climb anymore."

Soon, a year had passed. Teacher Turtle once again told the class about the rock climbing contest. Everyone was super excited, except for one — Garrett. He didn't want to join again, **ever**.

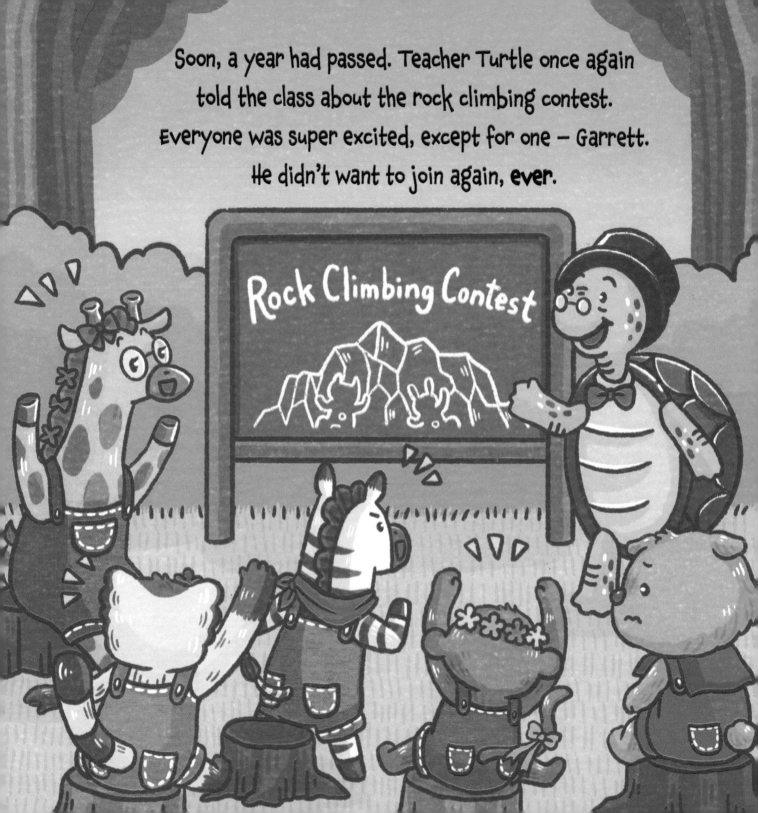

Rock Climbing Contest

That night at dinner, Mama Bear asked, "I heard from Zchool today. Will you join the contest again this year?"
Garrett shook his head and said "No, Mama. Never ever!"

Mama and Papa Bear both looked at each other, but they didn't say a thing.

The next morning, Papa Bear asked Garrett a question when they went fishing. "My son, **do you know what failure is?**" Garrett shook his head.

Failure is when you fail at something or when you didn't succeed or reach your goal.

I don't like that, Papa.

Papa smiled and answered, “Me either. Nobody likes to fail, my son.

When I fail, I often feel:

Papa remembered when he was young and told Garrett, "Yes, my son. In fact, **I failed many many times** before I became the champion."

"I remember I was just as sad as you are. I, too, wanted to give up rock climbing."

"Failure itself is harsh and often makes us emotional. If we hold onto it for long, it'd be like holding onto many big rocks. It's very heavy and makes us want to give up."

"But itis not an end point. When we learn from each failure and keep trying, we build a path and keep moving forward to **the land of success**!

"But Papa, how can I learn? How do I go to the land of success?" Garrett was still concerned.

Papa patiently answered, "Good question. Here are five steps that might help."

Five Steps to Handle Failure

1. Take a breath, calm down

2. Remember it's okay to fail

Failure happens. It is NOT the end point.

3. Learn from failure

What went wrong? What can I do better?

4. Make a new plan

5. Try again when ready!

Can you remember these steps with Garrett?

The next morning, even though Garrett felt nervous, he went to Teacher Turtle and put his name down for the rock climbing contest.

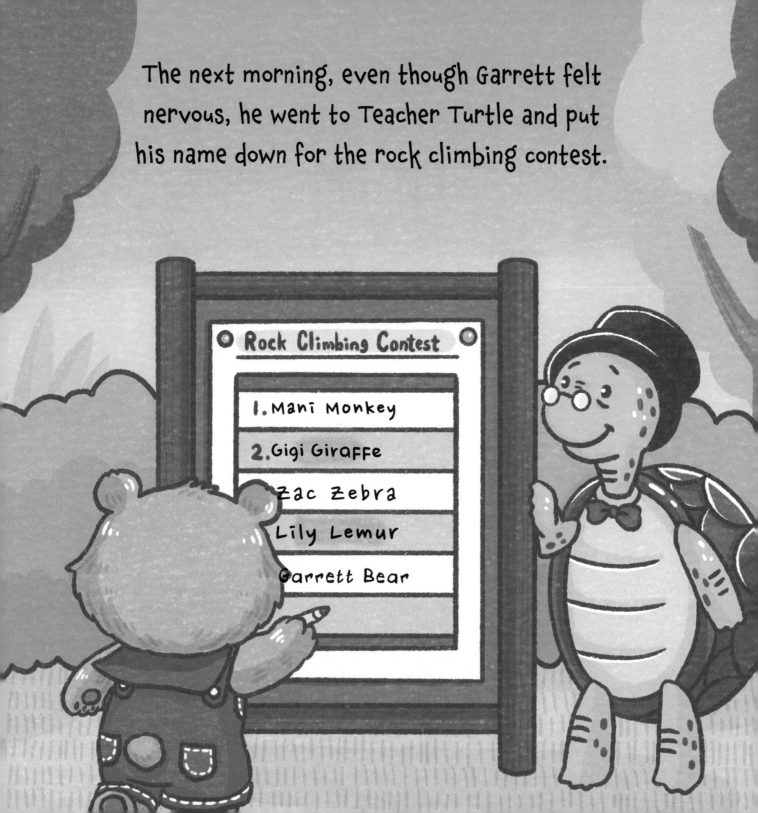

Rock Climbing Contest

1. Mani Monkey
2. Gigi Giraffe
   Zac Zebra
   Lily Lemur
   Garrett Bear

Back at home, Garrett thought about why he failed last time. He realized maybe it was because he hadn't had enough time to practice, and wasn't strong enough.

This time, he made a few changes to his plan and created a new one, a **better plan**, for his practice.

In the training field, Garrett only experienced **more failures.**

He **slipped**, he fell,

he **struggled** to hang on.

But he always remembered what Papa taught him —learn from each failure and keep trying. With practice, he only got better at climbing and his muscles became stronger.

When Sports Day finally came, even Garrett felt nervous,
he felt truly ready because he knew he had practiced enough.

After Teacher Turtle blew the whistle, Garrett moved quickly and swiftly. He climbed higher and higher bit by bit.

Soon, he was in the lead!

With only a few meters left to the top, Garret felt **exhausted**. His muscles started to burn.

He was feeling weaker and weaker. He wanted to stop...

But a voice within cheered loudly, "Don't give up yet! Keep going a little bit more! I can do this!"

Garrett took a deep breath and used all of the energy
he had left to continue to climb a little bit more.

3 more teps... 2 more steps... 1 last step!

Finally, Garrett reached the top! He had **succeeded** and became the new **rock climbing champion** of Character Zchool! He felt extremely proud of himself and so was everyone else.

Ever since then, whenever Garrett faced a challenge and failed, he looked at the trophy and remembered the steps to reajust and overcome failures.

Do you still remember the 5 steps to overcome failures?

Guide for Parents, Caregivers & Educators

Most children are afraid to fail. However, kids can never build perseverance unless they learn how to deal with failure. As parents and educators, we can help them recognize that failure is part of the path to success and here are some more tips for you:

1. Acknowledge what happened and the feelings

Talk about what happened without criticizing or shaming. Help your child identify the complex emotions they are feeling about failure (sadness, disappointment, frustration etc) and teach them what they can do to calm down.

2. Recognize their effort

Give as much praise for their effort as we do for a winning outcome. Point out what they did well. (e.g. "I see you trying hard and running really well on the field. I feel proud to see that.")

3. Remind them what failure means

Feel free to go through some pages in this story to remind them that failure is not the end point.

4. Think about next time, make a new plan

Reflect on their "failure" experience: What they did well, what didn't go so well, what they can do better. Remind them now that they know better, they are able to do better next time.

5. Teach self-pep talk

Use the **activity sheet on the next page** to help your child brainstorm his/her own personal phrases about perseverance at the moment of challenge. Encourage them to repeat it often until he/she can use it alone. Short, postitive statements like, "I can learn from my mistake!" "I can do this!"

6. Give them deliberate practice time

Give children enough time to develop specific aspects of their strength and be intentional about it.

Failures are the building blocks for success!

What can you say to yourself when youre facing failures? Write them down in the bubbles below!

About the Author

K. Tang is a former teacher who has years of experience in **character education**. She believes character education plays a vital role in helping children develop their **full potential** and enable them to gain the **social- emotional tools** to succeed in society. She hopes this series will encourage and empower storytellers to be educators of character for their children! Follow her on social media for more information and parenting tips!

Instagram Pages:
@k.tang.official

About the Illustrator

Michelle C. is a talented, independent illustrator based in Hong Kong as well as Canada. Playful and soft are the keywords that characterize her work. Her illustrations reflect her innocent, inner-child like personality. Follow her on social media for more of her work!

Instagram Page:
@ charlielomou